American edition published in 2015 by Andersen Press USA, an imprint of Andersen Press Ltd.

www.andersenpressusa.com

First published in Great Britain in 2015 by

Andersen Press Ltd., 20 Vauxhall Bridge Road, London SW1V 2SA.

Published in Australia by Random House Australia Pty.,

Level 3, 100 Pacific Highway, North Sydney, NSW 2060.

Copyright © Tony Ross, 2014.

Distributed in the United States and Canada by Lerner Publishing Group, Inc.

241 First Avenue North Minneapolis, MN 55401 U.S.A.

For reading levels and more information, look up this title at www.lernerbooks.com.

Color separated in Switzerland by Photolitho AG, Zürich.

Printed and bound in Malaysia by Tien Wah Press.

Library of Congress Cataloging-in-Publication Data Available.

ISBN: 978–1–4677–5797–3

ISBN: 978–1–4677–5798–0 (eBook)

A Little Princess Story

I Feel Sick!

Tony Ross

Andersen Press USA

The Little Princess was never sick.

Except when anyone asked her to do something.

"Why not take Scruff for a walk?" said the King.

"Ooooh, I feel sick!" said the Little Princess.

"Can you help me clean out the cat's box?" asked the Queen.

"I'd really enjoy that," said the Little Princess. "But I feel sick!"

"Will you help me teach my horse to jump?" asked the General.

"I would love to help," said the Little Princess. "But I feel sick!"

The Little Princess felt most sick when it was time to go to school. "You don't *look* sick," said the Queen.

So the Little Princess painted her face green.

"I can hardly walk," she said. "I feel so sick!"

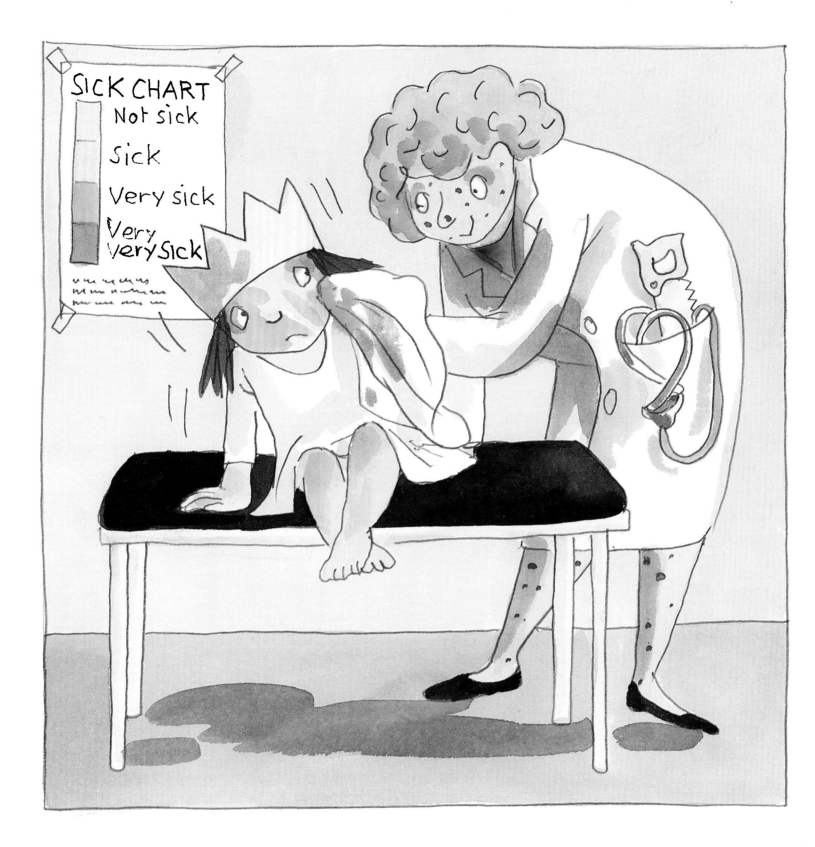

"Eat vegetables for dinner, that's the thing!"
said the Doctor. "Lots of greens will make you less green."

"I feel too sick to eat any dinner," said the Little Princess.
"But I might just manage a few jelly beans."

One day, when the Little Princess felt far too sick to do
anything at all, the postman brought her a letter.

"Ooooh!" she squealed. "It's an invitation to Molly's party!"

"Pity you can't go," said the Queen. "You feel too sick."

"I feel MUCH better now!" said the Little Princess.

The day of the party arrived. The Little Princess felt so excited.
"Don't you feel sick?" asked the Maid.

"No," said the Little Princess. "I feel WONDERFUL!"

The party was fun and there was so much to eat!

There were games to play and lots of dancing . . .

"Oh, no!" said the Little Princess.

"I feel sick!"

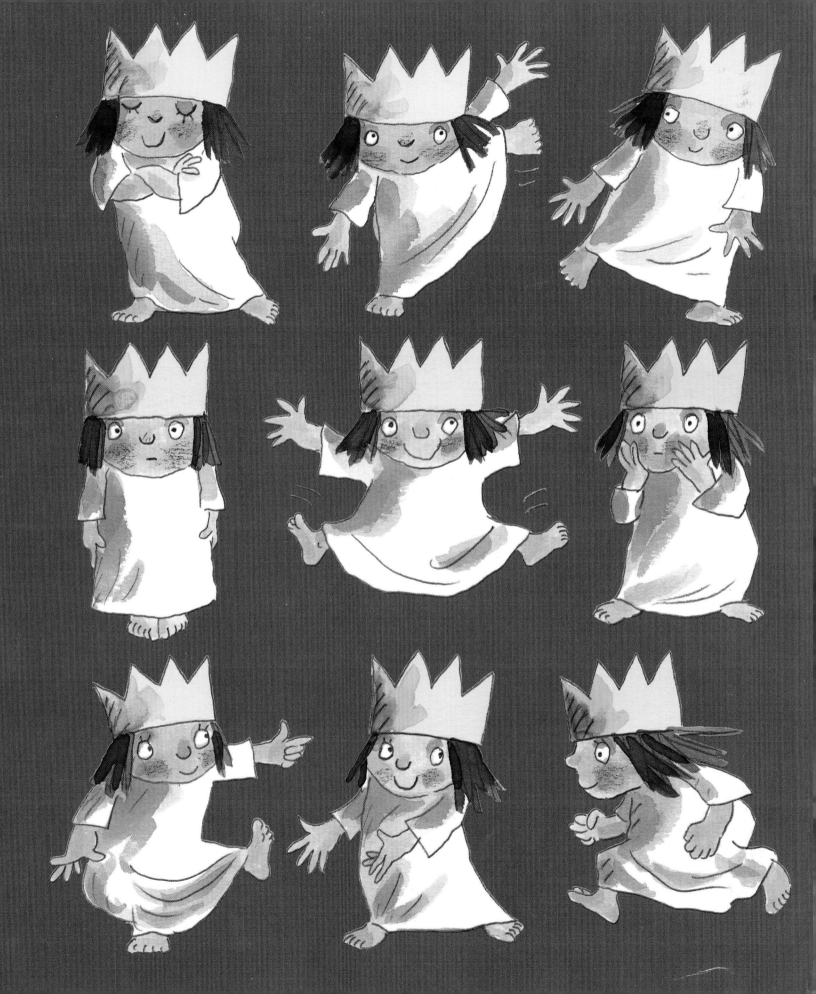